Prince Rama
and the
Demon King

by Damian Harvey and Manuel Šumberac

FRANKLIN WATTS
LONDON•SYDNEY

Prince Rama
and the
Demon King

Contents

Chapter 1

The House of Light

As Dad drove him to Sanjeeva's house, Joe couldn't help feeling nervous. He hadn't been to his friend's home before and wasn't sure what to expect, especially as there would be so many people there.

In school, they'd been learning about Diwali, the Hindu festival of lights, and Sanjeeva's mum, Mrs Varma, had come in to help them make samosas. The samosas had tasted delicious and Joe wished there were more of them.

That's when Mrs Varma invited him round for the evening. Joe had been uncertain about joining his friend's family for such an important celebration, but Mrs Varma insisted. "Diwali is a time of celebration for family and friends," she said. "You'll be most welcome."

4

"There'll be more samosas," Sanjeeva promised. "And

Grandpa Ramesh will be telling the story of Rama and

the Demon King. You don't want to miss that."

So Joe had agreed and Dad offered to drop him off and

pick him up later in the evening.

They turned off the main road. Dad began to drive slowly,

peering out of the window at each house as they passed by.

"What number does Sanjeeva live at?"

"I can't remember," Joe admitted. "But he said we won't be

able to miss it."

With only a few streetlamps to light the way, the road was

quite dark.

"We can't see the house numbers anyway," said Dad.

"Perhaps you should give him a call."

"No need," Joe replied. "I think I can see his house now."

Up ahead, one of the houses stood out amongst

the others.

The curtains were wide open and light was spilling out on to the pavement. As Dad pulled up outside, they could see rows of candles in the windows. There were even candles leading up to the front door.

"Did you know that Diwali means 'row of lights'?" said Joe. Dad laughed. "I'm impressed," he said. "It's good to see you've remembered *something* you learnt in school."
"Ha ha! Very funny," said Joe, climbing out of the car. As Dad drove away, Joe headed up the path towards the house. Before he had chance to knock, the door flew open and Sanjeeva's dad welcomed him in.

"Happy Diwali, Joe," he said. "It's good you're joining us. Sanji's in the kitchen with Nisha. Probably eating all the food, knowing him."

Joe grinned and headed into the kitchen where Sanjeeva was helping his mum with the food. "Happy Diwali, Sanji," he said. "Happy Diwali, Mrs Varma."

Before shooing them out of the kitchen, Sanjeeva's mum insisted that he call her Nisha. "You're not in school now, you know."

On the floor in the front room, Joe spotted a pattern made up of flower petals and brightly coloured sands. Small candles set around its edges made it flicker and dance with life.

"It's a Rangoli," explained Sanjeeva. "It's to welcome in the gods and bring good luck."

"I've never seen so many candles," said Joe.

"Diwali is the festival of lights," Sanjeeva reminded him.

"But wait until later … we've got fireworks, too."

"Cool!" said Joe. "I can't wait."

"I'm afraid you must," said Sanjeeva's dad. "The food's ready."

Joe had forgotten how hungry he was. He piled his plate

high with samosas and delicious vegetable curry.

After eating, everyone gathered in the front room, some

sitting on chairs and others on cushions on the floor.

When everyone was ready, Grandpa Ramesh began

his story …

Chapter 2

Rama and Sita

Many years ago, in the Indian city of Ayodhya, there lived a great king named Dashratha. As the king was getting old, he needed to decide which of his four sons would take his place on the throne.

For Dashratha, the decision was easy. Prince Rama was the natural heir to the throne. Not only was he the eldest, but he was brave, honest and handsome. The prince had also recently married Sita – a beautiful, kind and clever princess. Knowing that the people of Ayodhya loved Rama and Sita, Dashratha felt sure that, together, they would make great rulers.

On hearing the news, the people celebrated in the streets. It seemed that everyone was happy with Dashratha's decision … but this wasn't quite so.

Kaikeyi, one of King Dashratha's three wives, was angry and jealous. She wanted her son, Bharat, to become king. Bharat was Prince Rama's half-brother. He was younger than Rama and had never expected nor wanted to be chosen as king. However, his mother Kaikeyi had a plan. Many years before, Kaikeyi had saved King Dashratha's life. The king had been so grateful that he'd promised to grant his wife two wishes.

Instead of using the wishes right away, Kaikeyi had shrewdly held on to them, knowing that they would prove more useful at a later date.

Now as she made her way through the palace, a smile slowly spread across Kaikeyi's face. She knew that it was time to have her wishes granted.

Dashratha welcomed his wife, remembering his promise. "Anything you wish for shall be yours," he told her.

"First, I wish for you to send Rama and Sita away to live in the jungle for fourteen years," Kaikeyi told him. "Second, I wish for you to make our son, Bharat, king of Ayodhya."

On hearing these wishes, King Dashratha slumped down on to his throne and shook his head sadly, but he knew that he had no choice.

He was an honourable man and he could never break a promise.

When he told Rama what had happened, the prince nodded his head. "I understand," he said to his father. "Sita and I will go and live with people in the jungle. I'm sure that Bharat will make a good king."

Bharat was shocked when he heard what his mother had done. He ran to Rama and begged him to stay.

"I cannot," said Rama. "A promise is a promise."

"Then give me a pair of your sandals," said Bharat. Rama was puzzled, but he took off his sandals and handed them to his half-brother.

Bharat carefully placed the sandals on the royal throne.

"They will stay there until you return," he said. "Then the people will remember that it's you who is the rightful king of Ayodhya."

Stepping forward, Lakshmana, another of Dashratha's sons, placed his hand on Rama's shoulder. "I will come with you, and I will make sure you do return," he said. "Not only are you my brother, but you are also my best friend. The jungle is full of demons, and you will need me by your side."

* * *

Grandpa Ramesh broke off from telling the story for a moment to have a drink of his tea. While he did, Sanjeeva and Joe took the opportunity to go and grab a couple more samosas from the other room.

"It's a cool story," said Joe. "But I can't help feeling sorry for Rama and Sita."

"Wait until you hear what happens next," replied his friend. "Come on ... we don't want to miss anything."

The two boys got back into the front room just in time. Grandpa Ramesh was ready to continue.

Chapter 3

Into the Jungle

Leaving the palace and their life of comfort and luxury far behind them, Rama, Sita and Lakshmana journeyed for many days until they reached the jungle. It was here that they would have to find themselves a new home.

After trekking through dense undergrowth and along winding, narrow pathways, the three travellers eventually found themselves at the edge of a small village.

The villagers were overjoyed to see Rama, Sita and Lakshmana and greeted them as friends. They told them that they were welcome to live in their humble village for as long as they wanted. But they also told them about Ravana, the evil Demon King.

"Ravana is terrible," said the head of the village. "He has ten heads and twenty arms."

"His eyes are the colour of a burning red fire," another villager told them. "And he rides on a chariot that's pulled through the skies by ferocious flesh-eating mules."

The villagers told them how Ravana made their lives miserable. "He sends his demons to attack our village, ruining our peaceful lives and disrupting our thoughts and prayers," they said. "Will you help us, mighty princes?"

Rama nodded. "Fear not," he told the villagers. "Lakshmana and I will protect you from those demons."

Living in the jungle was very different to their old lives in
the busy palace with all its hustle and bustle. In the village,
it was peaceful and quiet and they soon began to enjoy
a more simple life together.

But the peace didn't last and it wasn't long before Ravana's
demons returned to attack the village and terrorise
the people. But this time, Rama and Lakshmana were ready.

As soon as the horde of demons appeared, Prince Rama
and his brother took up their weapons, ready to defend
the village and its people. The demons weren't used to
anyone fighting back and they fled in fear but, knowing that
they would surely return, Rama and Lakshmana chased
after them through the jungle.

No matter how hard they fought, the demon horde could
not defeat Rama and Lakshmana. It wasn't long before
the two heroes had chased all the demons out of
the jungle.

King Ravana was furious when his demon army told him

that Rama and Lakshmana had defeated them.

"They were too brave and powerful for us,"

protested one of the demon warriors.

"I will go and teach these mortals a lesson myself,"

Ravana roared.

The king was determined to make the princes pay for defeating his demons. He felt sure that the two of them would be no match for him in battle.

With a crack of his whip and a snap of the mules' sharp teeth, King Ravana's chariot flew high into the air and amongst the clouds.

The Demon King peered down in search of Rama, Sita and Lakshmana. Then, soaring over the jungle, he came in sight of the peaceful little village that his demons had told him about.

First he saw Rama and Lakshmana, and then he spotted Rama's beautiful wife, Sita. An evil plan formed in his head, and the Demon King smiled to himself. He would capture Sita and take her back to be one of his wives.

***

Grandpa Ramesh reached for his tea cup again.

"But you can't stop there," cried Joe.

Everyone laughed and Joe felt his face turn bright red with embarrassment.

"Storytelling is thirsty work," Grandpa laughed.

While Grandpa Ramesh finished his drink, Joe shivered at the thought of the twenty-armed Demon King riding across the sky in his chariot with the flesh-eating mules snapping their sharp teeth. He couldn't help wondering what on earth Rama, Sita and Lakshmana could do to stop him.

Chapter 4

The Demon King's Plan

*The next morning, as Sita was fetching water
from the river, she caught sight of a golden deer
running through the jungle.*

*"Did you see that?" she asked
her husband. "It was the most
beautiful creature I have ever seen."*

Sita was about to follow the deer, but Rama stopped her.

*"No!" he said. "Even without the demons, the jungle is
a dangerous place. Stay here. Lakshmana and I will go
in search of the creature."*

*Rama and his brother followed the deer's tracks into
the jungle, but each time they got close, it seemed to
vanish before their eyes. So deeper and deeper they went.*

Back in the village, Sita was waiting for her husband
to return when an old man came by their house.
The old man looked kind and friendly so the princess
went out to talk to him.

"Do you have some water so I might quench my thirst?"
asked the old man. "And a chair where I can sit and rest
for a while."

Sita was kind and generous, so without thinking she ran
inside to fetch a cup of water. When she returned,
the man grabbed Sita by the wrist, making
her cry out in pain.

"Let go," she cried. "My husband
will be here soon."

"Your foolish husband is deep
in the forest, searching for
golden deer," hissed the old man.
"You are mine now."

Sita struggled but, as she did, the man transformed before her very eyes. Instead of a harmless old man, Sita now saw the ten-headed Demon King, Ravana.

Sita cried for help but Ravana was too strong and the villagers were afraid to leave their houses. Sweeping the princess up in his arms, the Demon King carried her to his golden chariot, where the mules waited kicking their hooves and baring their sharp teeth.

"You can forget about your handsome prince," laughed the Demon King. "When we return to my home island of Lanka, you will become my wife."

Sita knew she wasn't strong enough to escape from the Demon King, but she was clever. As the chariot took to the air, she slipped a golden ring from her finger and, being careful not to let Ravana see, let it fall to the floor. Next, the princess removed her bracelets, one by one, and let the colourful gems fall to the ground below.

Later that day, when Rama and Lakshmana returned home, there was no sign of Sita. Then Prince Rama spotted something on the floor.

"Look!" he said, holding it up for Lakshmana to see. "This ring belongs to Sita. She must have dropped it."

Then, thinking of the strange golden deer, Rama guessed what had happened.

"We've been tricked," he cried. "The Demon King has taken Sita."

"Then we are already too late," said Lakshmana. "His island home is a secret and we will never find him."

"Wait a minute," said Rama, running a little way into the jungle. "Here!" he cried. "This is a stone from the bracelet I gave Sita for her birthday."
Lakshmana smiled at his brother. "Your wife is clever as well as beautiful," he said. "I think she's left us a trail."

* * *

Once again, Grandpa Ramesh stopped talking and reached for his cup. "Oh dear," he said. "My cup's empty."
"Don't you worry," said Sanjeeva's mum. "I'll go and make you a fresh one."
Sanjeeva laughed and gave Joe a nudge. "Grandpa always does this," he whispered. "He says it helps build up tension."
"Well it certainly works," said Joe. "I can't wait to find out what happens next."

Chapter 5

Rama to the Rescue

Following the trail of gold and jewels that Sita had dropped,
Rama and Lakshmana made their way through the jungle.
After travelling for many miles, they arrived in the kingdom
of the monkeys and presented themselves to King Hanuman.
"Noble Hanuman," Rama said, bowing before the king.
"Ravana the Demon King has taken my beautiful wife, Sita.
Please help us find her."
"We must all stand up against the demons," Hanuman said,
and agreed that he and his army would track them down.
They all searched far and wide, but it was Hanuman himself
who spotted the Demon King's palace whilst flying over
the island of Lanka. He saw Sita sitting by a small pool,
crying, and landed on the ground by her feet.

"Do not worry Princess Sita," said Hanuman. "Your brave husband is coming to rescue you."

Hanuman raced back to tell Rama the good news and together, they raised an army of animals from the jungle. When the army reached the shore they looked across at the island of Lanka.

"How can we get across the water?" asked Lakshmana. "It is too deep and too wide."

But Hanuman had an idea.

"We will build a bridge," he said. "Then we can all cross safely."

Working together, the monkeys made themselves into a huge bridge that stretched from one side of the water to the other. When it was ready, the army marched across.

The battle raged for many days and nights. It was one of the biggest that anyone had ever seen. Rama, Lakshmana and the animals fought bravely, but it looked as though the ten-headed Demon King was going to win after all. Rama had just one chance left. Many years ago, the gods had rewarded him with a magical arrow that he could use in his time of need. Now, picking up his bow, Rama took careful aim as Ravana charged towards him waving twenty deadly swords in the air.

Just as the Demon King reached him, Rama loosed the magical arrow. With a mighty whoosh, the arrow flew straight at Ravana, sinking deep into his heart. With a crash that shook the ground, Ravana fell down dead at Rama's feet.

After the great battle, Rama, Sita and Lakshmana returned to the village where they lived peacefully until their fourteen years of exile had passed and it was time for them to return home. The night had fallen by the time they left the jungle and it was so dark that the three travellers found it difficult to see which way to go.

Sita saw a light flickering in the distance. "Look," she said. "A light to guide us home."

As they got closer to the city, they saw that every window flickered with candlelight and the streets were illuminated by thousands more.

"Now our way is clear," said Rama, taking his wife

by the hand. "Out of the darkness and into the light."

As they entered the city, people came out of their houses

to welcome Rama, Sita and Lakshmana. Up ahead, Rama's

brother, Bharat, was waiting to lead them into the palace.

"Welcome home, my brother," said Bharat, returning

Rama's sandals to him and bowing. "My king."

The people cheered as Rama and Sita took their rightful

place on the throne, and there they ruled for many years

with kindness and wisdom.

* * *

Grandpa Ramesh smiled at Joe as he finished his story.

"And from that day onwards we have celebrated Diwali

so we remember the return of Rama and Sita," he said.

"The victory of light over darkness and good over evil."

Things to think about

1. Why do you think Joe is nervous about going to Sanjeeva's house at the beginning of the story?
2. How does Grandpa Ramesh build up the tension in the story?
3. Think about the themes in the story, such as the battle of light over darkness and love. What is the most important theme in your opinion?
4. How is Rama able to defeat Ravana? Would he have been able to do this alone?
5. What does the welcome Rama and Sita received from Bharat tell us about him?

Write it yourself

This book tells the story of Diwali. Now try to write your own story that explains a festival you know about.

You could feature a festival that you celebrate, or a different festival.

Plan your story before you begin to write it.

Start off with a story map:

• a beginning to introduce the characters and where and when your story is set (the setting);

• a problem which the main characters will need to fix in the story;

• an ending where the problems are resolved.

Get writing! Try to include geographical and historical details so that your readers get a sense of the time and place of your story, and think about the dialogue your characters would use. Would they use formal or informal language?

Notes for parents and carers

Independent reading
The aim of independent reading is to read this book with ease. This series is designed to provide an opportunity for your child to read for pleasure and enjoyment. These notes are written for you to help your child make the most of this book.

About the book
When Joe goes to his friend Sanjeeva's house to celebrate Diwali, Grandpa Ramesh tells them the story of Rama and Sita, and how they and Lakshmana defeated the terrible demon king Ravana.

Before reading
Ask your child why they have selected this book. Look at the title and blurb together. What do they think it will be about? Do they think they will like it?

During reading
Encourage your child to read independently. If they get stuck on a longer word, remind them that they can find syllable chunks that can be sounded out from left to right. They can also read on in the sentence and think about what would make sense.

After reading
Support comprehension by talking about the story. What happened?
Then help your child think about the messages in the book that go beyond the story, using the questions on the page opposite. Give your child a chance to respond to the story, asking:
Did you enjoy the story and why? Who was your favourite character?
What was your favourite part? What did you expect to happen at the end?

Franklin Watts
First published in Great Britain in 2019
by The Watts Publishing Group

Series Editors: Jackie Hamley and Melanie Palmer
Series Advisors: Dr Sue Bodman and Glen Franklin
Series Designer: Peter Scoulding

A CIP catalogue record for this book is
available from the British Library.

ISBN 978 1 4451 6537 0 (hbk)
ISBN 978 1 4451 6538 7 (pbk)
ISBN 978 1 4451 7040 4 (library ebook)

Printed in China

Franklin Watts
An imprint of
Hachette Children's Group
Part of The Watts Publishing Group
Carmelite House
50 Victoria Embankment
London EC4Y 0DZ

An Hachette UK Company
www.hachette.co.uk

www.franklinwatts.co.uk

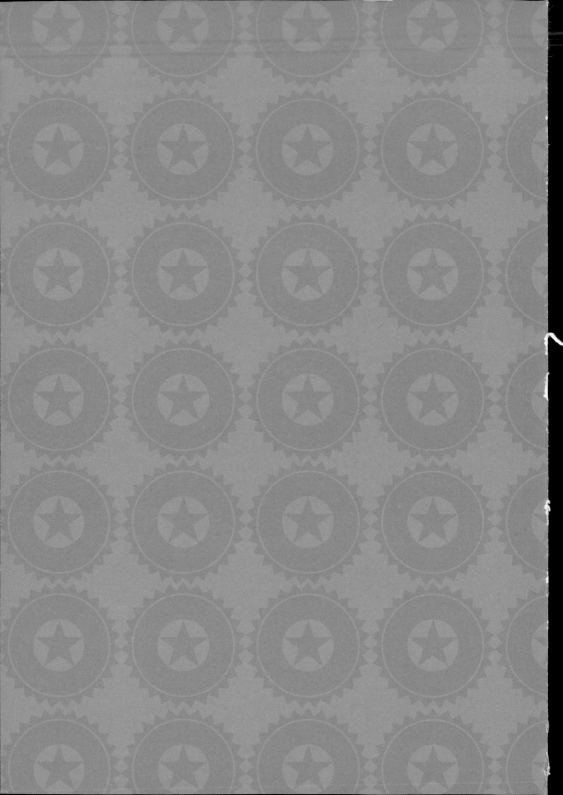